THE 156-STOREY TREEHOUSE

BY

ANDY GRIFFITHS

& TERRY DENTON

MACMILLAN CHILDREN'S BOOKS

First published 2022 by Pan Macmillan Australia Pty Limited

First published in the UK 2022 by Macmillan Children's Books
an imprint of Pan Macmillan
The Smithson, 6 Briset Street, London EC1M 5NR
EU representative: Macmillan Publishers Ireland Ltd, 1st Floor,
The Liffey Trust Centre, 117–126 Sheriff Street Upper
Dublin 1, D01 YC43
Associated companies throughout the world
www.panmacmillan.com

ISBN 978-1-5290-8859-5

Text copyright © Backyard Stories 2022
Illustrations copyright © Terry Denton 2022

The right of Andy Griffiths and Terry Denton to be identified as the
author and illustrator of this work has been asserted by them
in accordance with the Copyright, Designs and Patents Act 1988.

1 3 5 7 9 8 6 4 2

A CIP catalogue record for this book is available from the British Library.

Printed and bound by CPI Group (UK) Ltd, Croydon CR0 4YY

CONTENTS

CHAPTER 1

THE 156-STOREY TREEHOUSE

Hi, my name is Andy.

1

This is my friend Terry.

We live in a tree.

Well, when I say 'tree', I mean treehouse. And when I say 'treehouse', I don't just mean any old treehouse—I mean a 156-*storey* treehouse. (It used to be a 143-storey treehouse, but we've added another 13 storeys.)

So what are you waiting for?
Come on up!

We've added a bouldering alley (it's just like bowling, except you use boulders instead of balls),

a wishing well,

an aquarium wonderland (home of Quazjex the
stunt axolotl),

lost
sausage

an old boot camp,

an enigma engine,

a world record breaking level,

15

the amazing mind-reading sandwich-making machine (it knows exactly what sort of sandwich you want and makes it for you),

a TV quiz show level hosted by Quizzy the quizzical quizbot,

a lost property office,

a lost sausage office,

Spoontopia,

a super-stinky stuff level

PETROL

Hee, hee!

Hairy old Gorgonzola cheese

WET DOG

Smelly old swamp

OLD DEAD BIRD

Smelly pig

23-day old milk

Smelly pig sty mud box

and a Billions of Birds™ level.

As well as being our home, the treehouse is where we make books together. I write the words and Terry draws the pictures.

As you can see, we've been doing this for quite a while now.

Things can get a bit crazy from time to time …

but we always get our book done in the end!

CHAPTER 2

HAPPY HOLIDAYS

If you're like most of our readers, you're probably wondering what holidays we celebrate in the treehouse.

Well, we celebrate all the holidays there are—and even some there aren't!

Take-A-Chance Day

Kiss-A-Frog Day

Underpants-On-Your-Head Day

Cow-Over-The-Moon Day

Popping-Popcorn-With-The-Lid-Off Day

Christmas Day

Jump-Off-A-Mountain Day

Chair-Up-Your-Nose Day

My and Terry's Birthday

Jill's Birthday

He, he!

Heehee!

Gingerbread Day

BEEP! BEEP!

Swallow-A-Car Day

Easter

Stay-In-Bed-All-Day Day

Sorry! Just can't do it...

Be-Nice-To-Andy-All-Day Day

Big
Bad
Wolf
Day

'Hey,' says Terry. 'Remember how last year on Big Bad Wolf Day that big bad wolf came to the treehouse and said, "Andy and Terry, let me come in!"

 'And we said, "No, no, not by the hair on our chinny-chin-chins."

'But the wolf said, "I'll huff and I'll puff and I'll BLOW your treehouse down!"

'And then he huffed …

Air in

'and he puffed …

39

41

'How could I forget?' I say. 'Especially since exactly the same thing happens *every* year on Big Bad Wolf Day.'

 'And remember that time on Gingerbread Day,' says Terry, 'when we made a gingerbread Terry,

'and a gingerbread Andy,

'and a gingerbread Jill,

'and how they were cooling down on the tray when suddenly they all jumped up and said, "Run, run as fast you can, you can't catch us, we're the Gingerbread Gang!"

'And we ran …

'and we ran …

HEE, HEE.

Gingerbread crumbs

'and we ran …

'and we ran …

45

'and we ran …

'and we ran …

 'and we ran as fast as we could, but they were right—we couldn't catch them!'

'How could I forget?' I say. 'The same thing happens *every* year on Gingerbread Day.'

'I've got an idea,' says Terry. 'How about next Gingerbread Day we make gingerbread cars as well, and then when the Gingerbread Gang run away, we'll be able to catch them!'

'Great plan,' I say. 'We'll definitely do that *next* Gingerbread Day, but tonight, in case you've forgotten, is the night before Christmas, and we've still got a lot to do.'

more christmas lights

christmas lights

'I haven't forgotten,' says Terry. 'I've been working on the Christmas lights.'

'How many have you done so far?' I say.

'Um,' says Terry, 'let me see. Six million, fifty-five thousand, four hundred and eighty-nine. One for each leaf!'

'And how many have you got to go?'

'One,' says Terry. 'I'll just do it now.'

Terry
climbs
to the
top rung
of the
ladder
and
places
a light
on the
only
leaf
that
doesn't
already
have
one.
'Ta da!'
he says.

light

leaf

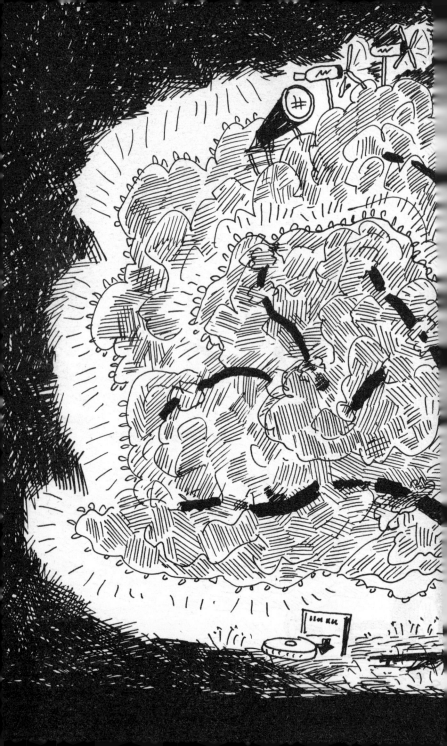

'Great job!' I say. 'The tree looks really Christmassy!'

'Thanks, Andy,' says Terry. He slides down the ladder and lands beside me. 'I LOVE Christmas.'

'Me too,' I say.

Frog

CHAPTER 3

MR BIG NOSE CALLING

In case you don't know, that's the sound of our 3D video phone. It's what our publisher, Mr Big Nose, always calls on to remind us that our next book is due.

'Don't answer it, Andy!' says Terry. 'It's probably Mr Big Nose calling to remind us that our next book is due.'

'Nah,' I say. 'We only just finished our last book and our next book isn't due for … um … er … actually I can't remember, but it's not for *ages*!'

'Then he must be ringing to wish us Merry Christmas,' says Terry. 'Let's answer it!'

And before I can stop him, Terry answers the phone.

'What took you so long to answer?' says Mr Big Nose. 'I'm a busy man, you know!'

'We know,' I say, 'but we're busy, too—we're getting ready for Christmas.'

'Christmas?' says Mr Big Nose. 'Bah, humbug! I don't believe in Christmas—I'm too busy. I'm calling to remind you that your next book is due tomorrow!'

'Tomorrow?' I say.

'Tomorrow?' says Terry.

'TOMORROW!' says Mr Big Nose. 'I had to bring the deadline forward.'

'But tomorrow is *Christmas Day*!' I say.

'That's not important!' says Mr Big Nose. 'What's important is that it's the day your book is due!'

'No, you don't understand,' says Terry. 'It's *Christmas Day*. We'll be celebrating Christmas!'

'You'll be celebrating Christmas in the monkey house if you don't get your book written,' says Mr Big Nose.

'But we hate monkeys!' I say.

'Me too,' says Mr Big Nose. 'But you know what I hate even more? Not getting my book on time, that's what! A deadline is a deadline, so you'd better get it to me tomorrow, by 9 a.m., and not a moment later!'

The screen goes blank.

'But we *can't* write a book!' says Terry. 'It's getting late and we haven't written our letters to Santa yet.'

'*I* know,' I say. 'But Mr Big Nose doesn't care. You heard him: he doesn't even believe in Christmas. All he cares about is getting his book on time.'

'All right,' says Terry, sighing. 'But let's write our Santa letters first and *then* write our book.'

'I don't think that's such a good idea,' I say. 'We'll end up getting distracted—and when I say "we", I mean "you". *You* will end up getting distracted and we won't get our book done.'

lost
sausage

'I promise I won't get distracted,' says Terry. 'I definitely, positively, absolutely, totally, completely, utterly won't ... um ... er ... what was I saying again?'

'You were telling me that you won't get distracted,'
I say. 'But you got distracted in the middle of
telling me you wouldn't get distracted!'

'Sorry,' says Terry. 'What were you saying? Never
mind. Come on, Andy. Let's have a little fun. It's
Christmas!'

'I *know* it's Christmas,' I say. 'But I think we should do our book first, and write our Santa letters second.'

'No,' says Terry. 'I think we should do our book second and write our Santa letters first!'

'NO!' I shout. 'Book first—Santa letters second!'

'NO!' shouts Terry. 'Book second, Santa letters first!'

'Okay!' I say. 'You win—we'll do our Santa letters first and then write our book.'

'Yay!' says Terry. 'You won't regret it.'

'I will if we end up in the monkey house,' I say. 'I *hate* monkeys.'

'So do I,' says Terry. 'But I *love* Christmas!'

Birds

CHAPTER 4

LISTS, STOCKINGS AND CAROLS

We each grab a pencil and some paper.

'I'm not sure how to start,' says Terry.

I think for a moment. 'I'm going to write: *Dear Santa, I have been very good this year. For Christmas I would like …* and then just list all the things I want.'

'Me too!' says Terry, and he starts writing as fast as he can.

'I bet you can't guess what I put at the top of my list,' says Terry.

'Bet you I can,' I say.

'All right then,' says Terry. 'What?'

'An electric pony,' I say.

'That's right!' says Terry. 'But how did you know?'

'Because I read in your diary that that's what you want for Christmas,' I say.

'You shouldn't be reading my diary,' says Terry. 'It's private!'

'How was I supposed to know that?' I say.

'Because it says so on the cover!' says Terry. 'Look!'

'It doesn't have a lock on it,' I say.

'Then I'm going to add a top secret private diary lock to my Santa list,' says Terry.

'A lock won't stop *me*,' I say. 'I'll just ask Santa for a key to open it. And I'm also going to ask him for a *jet pack*!'

'Jet packs are cool,' says Terry. 'I'm going to ask for one, too.'

'But that's copying,' I say.

'No, it's not,' says Terry. 'Because I'm going to ask for an *invisible* jet pack.'

'Invisible jet pack?!' I say. 'I didn't even know there was such a thing. I'm going to add it to my list as well. Okay?'

'Sure,' says Terry. 'As long as you promise not to
ask Santa for a key to open my top secret private
diary lock.'

'Deal,' I say, adding an invisible jet pack to my
list. 'We can go invisible jet-packing together.'

'You'd better ask for an electric pony as well,'
says Terry. 'Just in case Santa doesn't come
through with the invisible jet packs.'

'Thanks,' I say. 'Good idea.'

We keep writing our lists. They get longer …

and longer ...

Ants!

and longer ...

and longer …

until we can't
think of anything
else to ask Santa for.

lost
sausage

77

'I think I'm finished,' says Terry.

'Me too,' I say. 'Our lists are quite long, though.
I hope Santa will be able to fit all these presents
into our Christmas stockings.'

ANTS!

'He sure will,' says Terry, 'thanks to these endlessly
expandable Christmas stockings I invented.
They're just like regular stockings, but no matter
how many presents you put into them, they keep
expanding!'

'High five!' I say to Terry. 'Let's hang up our endlessly expandable stockings and then get started on our book!'

'Wait!' says Terry. 'We haven't sung any Christmas carols yet!'

'There's no time!' I say.

'But we *always* sing Christmas carols on Christmas Eve,' says Terry. 'It's tradition!'

And before I can stop him, he starts singing at the top of his voice.

Jingle bells

Andy smells

Silky flew away

Father Christmas
lost his whiskers

And penguins ate his sleigh!

'Keep your voice down, Terry!' I say. 'If Santa hears you singing that you won't get any presents.'

'Why not?' says Terry.

'Because it's not a proper Christmas carol.'

'It's not?' says Terry.

'No!' I say. 'A proper Christmas carol is something like "The Twelve Days of Christmas".'

'All right, I'll sing that then,' says Terry.

On the first day of Christmas

My best friend gave to me

A penguin in a pear tree.

lost
sausage

83

On the second day of Christmas

My best friend gave to me

Two turtle-penguins

And a penguin in a pear tree.

On the third day of Christmas

My best friend gave to me

Three French penguins

Two turtle-penguins

And a penguin in
a pear tree.

On the fourth day of Christmas

My best friend gave to me

Four calling penguins

Three French penguins

Two turtle-penguins

And a penguin in a pear tree.

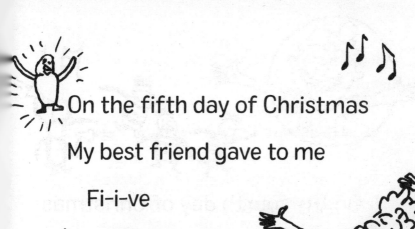

On the fifth day of Christmas

My best friend gave to me

Fi-i-ve

Gol-den

Pen-

'STOP!' I shout.

87

'What's the matter?' says Terry. 'You don't like that one?'

'No,' I say. 'Too many penguins!'

'Okay then,' says Terry. 'How about "Silent Night"?'

'Yes,' I say. 'That's a much better choice.'

Terry starts singing:

Silent night, holy night

Penguins are black

With a bit of white.

They like to eat fish

CHOMP!

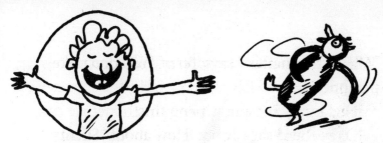

And they waddle about.

The slim ones are thin

And the fat
ones are stout.

Sleep in penguinly peace.

Sleep in penguinly peace.

89

'TERRY!' I shout. 'The sooner you stop singing penguin-themed Christmas carols, the sooner we can get our book written and the sooner we can get to bed and the sooner it will be Christmas.'

'Calm down, Andy,' says Terry. 'I've finished singing. The sooner you stop shouting, the sooner we can get our book written and the sooner we can get to bed and the sooner it will be Christmas! So stop shouting and let's get started right now!'

CHAPTER 5

THE MYSTERIOUS PRESENT

'Okay,' I say. 'How about we start the book with *Hi, my name is Andy*?'

'I've got a better idea,' says Terry. 'How about we start the book with *Hi, my name is—*'

DING DONG!

'*Hi, my name is Ding Dong*?' I say. 'What does that even mean? There's nobody called Ding Dong in the book.'

'I know,' says Terry. 'I didn't say *my name is—*'

'Yes you did!' I say. 'You just said it again!'

'I didn't!' says Terry. 'I was trying to say *my name is—*'

DING DONG!

'Yeah, I get what you're trying to tell me,' I say. '*Hi, my name is Ding Dong.* But I don't get it. Who's Ding Dong?'

'THE DOORBELL!' says Terry. 'There's somebody at the door—it might be Santa!'

'No,' I say. 'We're not asleep and, besides, he doesn't ring the doorbell, you—'

'That's not very nice,' says Terry. 'Calling me a ding dong.'

'I didn't call you a ding dong,' I say. 'It was the doorbell! I think there's somebody at the door.'

'I think you're right,' says Terry. 'Let's go and open it!'

We take the superfast slide down to the bottom of the tree …

and open the door.

Bill the Postman is standing there holding a large package.

lost sausage

Weee!!

'Merry Christmas, Andy and Terry,' he says. 'I love what you've done with the treehouse: it looks like there's a light on every single leaf!'

'That's because there *is*!' I say.

'Brilliant!' says Bill. 'Well, I've got a special delivery for you here. I don't know what it is, but it's very cold.'

'Thanks, Bill!' I say, taking the very cold parcel from him. 'See you at our treehouse Christmas party tomorrow.'

'Looking forward to it,' he says. 'See you then.'

We shut the door, carry the parcel upstairs and put it down in front of the fireplace.

'Who's it from?' says Terry.

'I don't know,' I say. 'There's no return address.'

'What do you think it is?'

'Maybe it's a present,' I say.

'Ooh goody!' says Terry. 'Let's open it.'

We tear the paper off. But underneath there's more paper. We rip that paper off, but underneath that there's even *more* paper!

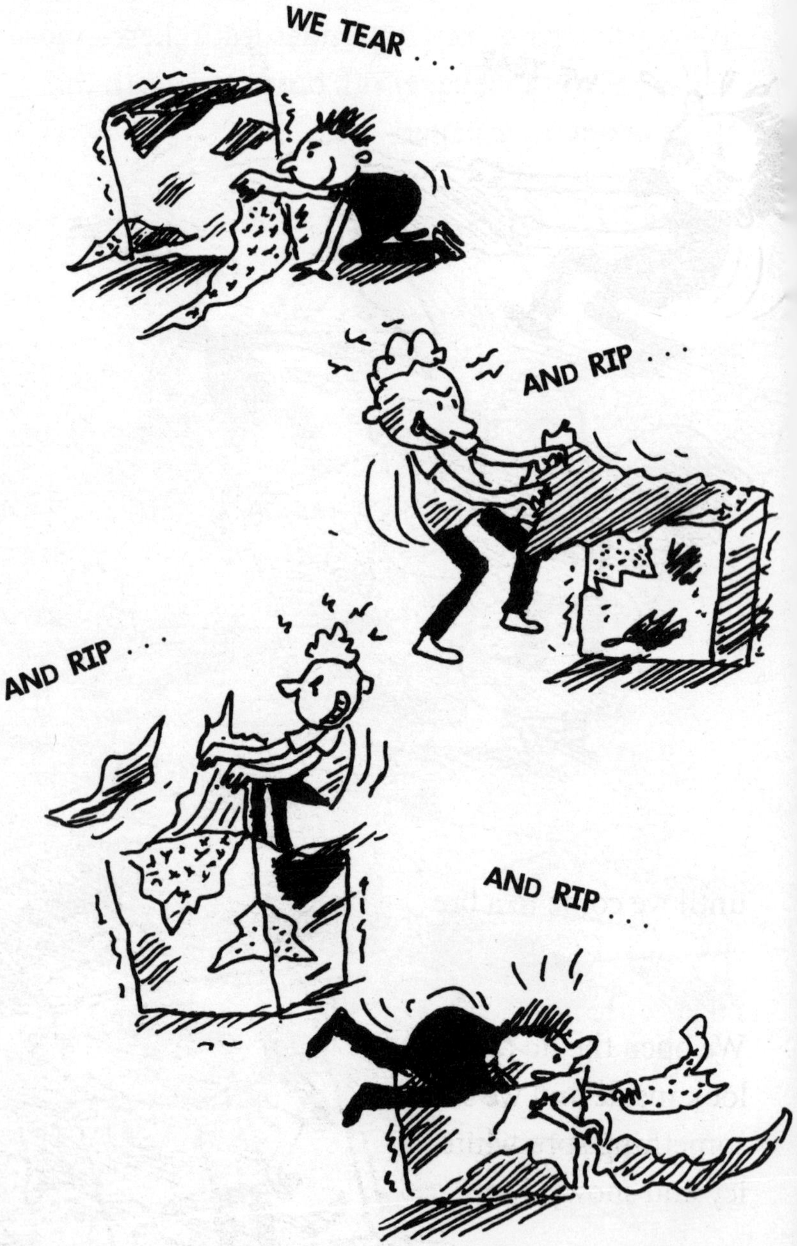
WE TEAR . . .
AND RIP . . .
AND RIP . . .
AND RIP . . .

WE TEAR . . .

WE TEAR . . .

until we come to a box.

We open the lid and
look inside and we see
something soft, white,
icy and snowy. It's . . .

A BOX FULL OF SOFT, WHITE, ICY-COLD SNOW!

'Yay!' says Terry. 'I *love* snow! Let's have a snowball fight!'

'Maybe later,' I say. 'We're supposed to be writing our book, remember?'

'Good point,' says Terry, 'but I think you're forgetting one thing.'

'What?' I say.

'To watch out for this!' says Terry, and he throws a snowball right at my head.

WHUMP!

It hits me in the face and snow goes all down the front of my shirt.

'Okay, you asked for it,' I say, gathering up the snow and returning fire.

We both race to the box to reload—

lost
sausage

and the great Christmas snowball fight begins!

We throw snowballs at each other until the box is completely empty.

There's snow all over the room now, which is good because it makes it look extra Christmassy. Santa's going to feel right at home.

'Hey, Andy!' says Terry. 'Let's make a Christmas snowman!'

'What about our book?' I say.

'We'll do it right after we make a snowman,' says Terry. 'It won't take long. Come on, help me roll the snow into balls.'

'Okay,' I say. 'But *then* we write the book.'

'Of course,' says Terry.

Soon we have three balls of snow—two big ones for the body and a small one for the head.

We put the head on top of the body,

and stick two small branches into the sides to make arms.

'Great!' says Terry. 'Now all it needs is a face.'

I push a carrot into the centre of the head. 'That's its nose!' I say.

'And these two pink marshmallows can be its eyes,' says Terry.

We add twigs for eyebrows and a jelly-snake mouth.

Terry's arm →

We wrap a scarf around its neck and put a big black hat on its head. Then we stand back to admire our Christmas snowman.

'What do you think?' says Terry.
  'I don't know,' I say. 'It looks kind of angry.'

'I think it's the eyebrows,' says Terry. 'They've slipped down a bit. I'll just fix them.'

lost
sausage

Terry straightens the eyebrows, but they sink down again, this time at a steeper angle, making the snowman look even angrier than before.

Terry reaches up to straighten the eyebrows again when, suddenly, the snowman opens its jelly-snake mouth and says in a gruff voice, 'Hey, kid, quit messin' with me brows! That's how I like 'em.'

CHAPTER 6

THE NOT-VERY-CHRISTMASSY SNOWMAN

Normally I like Christmas snowmen, but not this one—he's not very Christmassy at all.

'Nice joint you've got here,' says the snowman, swivelling his head around. 'Definitely better than where I come from. I think I'm going to like it here. Now get lost!'

'What do you mean "get lost"?' I say. 'We *live* here.'
    'You *used* to live here,' says the snowman. 'But it's my treehouse now.'

'No, it's not,' says Terry. 'It's *our* treehouse!'

'Yours?' says the snowman. 'That's a laugh. It doesn't belong to you. You made it out of the wood you stole from the wreck of Captain Woodenhead's pirate ship. I've read your books—I know *all* about you.'

'How could you possibly have read our books?'
I say. 'We only just made you.'

The snowman smiles with its jelly-snake mouth
and says, 'My grandmother used to read them to
me when I was just a little snowboy.

'That's why I wanted to come here. Your treehouse
looked like a lot more fun than standing around
freezing my base off in Antarctica.

'So I packed myself in a box and mailed myself here. I knew you two chuckleheads wouldn't be able to resist making a snowman out of a box of snow. And so, here I am!

'Don't forget to shut the door on your way out,' he says. 'Actually, on second thoughts, leave it open. It's quite warm in here. I think it's all those Christmas lights you've hung everywhere. Where's the off switch?'

'There is no off switch,' I say. 'It's Christmas, and if you don't like it, you can go right back to Antarctica—in fact, we'll help you. Terry, let's pack this snowman into his box and send him home.'

lost sausage

'Keep your hot little hands off me,' says the snowman, 'or I'll throw my head at you!'

'You don't scare me!' I say, advancing towards him.

'We'll see about that!' snarls the snowman. He reaches up with his twiggy arms, lifts his head off his body …

and hurls it right at us!

'I've got this!' yells Terry. He grabs our emergency snow shovel off the wall, steps in front of the hurtling head and takes a big swing at it.

WHAP!

It's a direct hit! The snowman's head breaks apart
and clumps of snow go flying in all directions.

'Snow long, snowman,' says Terry.

We high five, jump up and down, and do a victory
dance, stomping and splashing in the puddle
formed by the rapidly melting snow.

But then I hear a rumbling sound.

I turn around.

Uh-oh.

The snowman's body is hurtling towards us at high speed!

'Watch out, Andy!' shouts Terry.

'Don't worry!' I yell. 'I'll get *this* one.' I pull an emergency flamethrower from our emergency flamethrower dispenser, throw the switch to

EXTRA HOT

and start blasting.

lost
sausage

I keep blasting until the body
of the snowman is completely
melted. 'It was nice *snowing*
you,' I say. 'In fact, it's been
a real blast!'

'Let that be a lesson to
you!' says Terry. 'Now
you're nothing but a
harmless puddle.'

'That's what you think,' says the puddle. 'I'll get you for this—I vow never-ending revenge. You haven't heard the last of me!'

Suddenly the air is full of the sound of jingling bells.

'Oh no,' I say. 'It's Santa! He's coming!'

'But he can't come *now*,' says Terry. 'We're not asleep—and he only brings presents if you're asleep!'

'We'll just have to pretend,' I say. 'Quick! Lie down and shut your eyes.'

JINGLE JINGLE

CHAPTER 7

CRASH!

We throw ourselves to the floor and pretend to be asleep. Just in time! I can hear reindeer snorting, sleigh bells ringing and Santa HO-HO-HO-ing.

'Whoa, Rudolph!' calls Santa. 'Slow down, Donner, Blitzen, Vixen, Comet, Cupid, Dancer, Dasher and Prancer. Prepare for a landing in the treehouse down there—in that room where Andy and Terry are sleeping.'

'Santa Claus is going to land right *here*!' whispers Terry.

'I know,' I say. 'But I'm not sure it's the best place for a landing given there's an enormous puddle in the middle of the floor! I think we should warn him.'

'No!' says Terry. 'If we warn him, he'll know we're not asleep and he might not land at all. And if he doesn't land, we won't get any presents.'

'But if we don't warn him, he might crash,' I say.

'Are you trying to tell me that Santa doesn't know how to land his sleigh safely?' says Terry. 'Because I think he does—he's had a *lot* of practice.'

'Sure,' I say, 'but—'

'What just happened?' whispers Terry.

'I'm not sure,' I say. 'But judging by that CRASH, CRACK, TINKLE, BINGLE, TIMPLE, BASH, PLONK, KABOOM, FLOOP, BOING, KALUMP, SMASH, TWANG, FLONK, SNAP, PLOP, FLAP, DING, KLUNK, BARK, SPROING and BANG, I'd say Santa just crashed his sleigh.'

'Do you think we can open our eyes now?' says Terry.

'Yes,' I say.

We open our eyes and look around.

'Santa's not here,' says Terry.

'And neither are our presents,' I say. 'Our stockings are empty!'

'No, you're wrong, Andy,' says Terry, peering over the edge of the level. 'Look, there's a pony down there! Santa Claus brought me an electric pony!'

'That's not *an electric pony*!' I say. 'That's one of Santa's reindeer! Santa must have hit the puddle when he was landing and skidded over the edge.'

'I think you might be right,' says Terry. 'And it's not the only reindeer down there in the branches. There's lots of them!'

'But where's Santa?' I say.

'Look,' says Terry, pointing. 'He's landed on a branch just above the cloning machine level.'

'Oh no,' I say. 'That's quite a thin branch.'

'Yes,' says Terry. 'And Santa's quite a large man.'

'Yes,' I say. 'And quite heavy.'

'Do you think the branch will break?' says Terry.

'I hope not,' I say. 'But I'm pretty sure it will.'

There's a creaking sound …

followed by a cracking sound …

CRACK

the branch snaps …

SNAP

Santa falls …

FALL

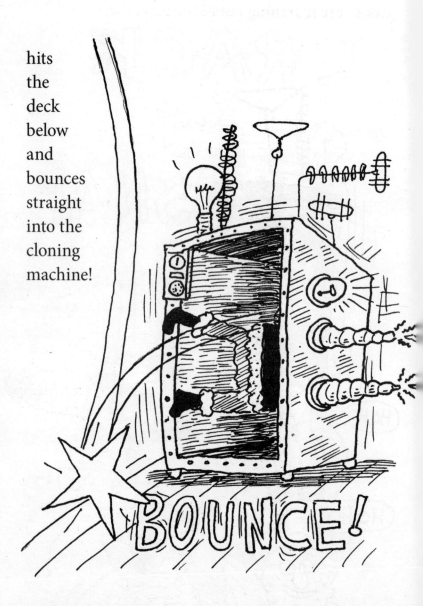

hits
the
deck
below
and
bounces
straight
into the
cloning
machine!

BOUNCE!

It whirrs to life, and within moments jolly Santa clones are marching out of the machine.

143

The Santas are all patting their bellies and saying,
'HO HO HO!'

'Wow!' says Terry. 'Look at all the Santas! Can we keep them, Andy? Can we?'

'Well, I guess we could,' I say, 'except we can't keep the *real* Santa. We have to let him go so he can finish delivering all his presents.'

'But which one *is* the real Santa?' says Terry. 'They all look exactly the same.'

'I guess we'd better go and ask them,' I say.

We climb down to the cloning machine level.
The Santas are very happy to see us.

'Merry Christmas, Andy and Terry!' they boom.

lost
sausage

'Merry Christmas and welcome to you all!' I say.
'It's great to have so many Santas in the treehouse,
but we were just wondering, which one of you is
the *real* Santa Claus?'

One of the Santas steps forward. *I'm* the real
Santa!' he says.

Another Santa shoves that Santa aside and says,
'No, *I'm* the real Santa!'

'Actually, I think you'll find that *I* am the real Santa,' says a third Santa, using his big round belly to bounce the other two Santas out of his way.

NCE!

The Santas continue to push and jostle one another, and their shouting gets louder and louder and louder, until there's only one thing left for me to do.

CHAPTER 8

QUIZZY GETS QUIZZING

'STOP SHOUTING!' I shout over the top of the shouting Santas. 'There's a better way to solve this than shouting!'

'There is?' shouts one of the Santas.

'Yes,' I say. 'A quiz. We'll get Quizzy the quizzical robot to ask you all questions that only the true Santa Claus would know the answers to, and then we'll know which one of you is the real Santa.'

'But I already told you,' shouts one of the Santas, '*I'm* the real Santa!'

'No, it's *me*!' shouts another.

'I think you'll find that it's ME,' shouts a third.

'ME! ME! ME!' shout the Santas.

'Okay, okay,' I say. 'Save it for the quiz. Come with us.'

With Terry leading the way, we climb up the tree to the TV quiz show level, and lead the Santas onto the set.

'Welcome!' says Quizzy. 'I'm your host, Quizzy the quizzical quizbot. Tonight's special subject is Santa Claus. Please take your places behind the desks, put your hands on the buzzers, and we'll begin!'

The Santas push and shove their way to the desks and soon they are all in position, ready to start the show.

'All right,' says Quizzy. 'Win 13 points for a correct answer. Lose 13 points for a wrong answer. First question: What is Santa's favourite colour?'

The sound of all the buzzers going off at the same time is deafening, as are the Santas when they all shout: 'RED!'

'You're *all* correct!' says Quizzy. 'That's 13 points each!'

'What is the name of Santa's favourite reindeer?'
says Quizzy.

'RUDOLPH!' shout the Santas.

'Correct!' says Quizzy.

'What is Santa's favourite drink?' says Quizzy.

'MILK!' shout the Santas.

'Correct!' says Quizzy.

'What is Terry hoping to get for Christmas?'
asks Quizzy.

'AN ELECTRIC PONY!' shout the Santas.

'Correct!' says Quizzy.

'Where does Santa live?' asks Quizzy.

'THE NORTH POLE!' shout the Santas.

'Correct!' says Quizzy.

'What size boots does Santa wear?' asks Quizzy.

'EXTRA LARGE!' shout the Santas.
 'Correct!' says Quizzy.

'What is the sound of Santa's laugh?' asks Quizzy.
  'HO HO HO!' shout the Santas.

'Correct!' says Quizzy.

'Are you the *real* Santa Claus?' asks Quizzy.

'YES!' shout the Santas.

'Correct!' says Quizzy.

'Well,' says Quizzy, 'it appears all our contestants are tied on 104 points! There's only one way to resolve this—a belly bounce-off! The last Santa standing will be the real Santa! Let the great belly bounce-off begin!'

The Santas all puff themselves up and begin belly bouncing one another as hard as they can.

171

lost sausage

172

The Santas belly bounce each other so hard, in fact, that they knock themselves out and all end up slumped in a big pile on the floor.

'Well, that didn't solve anything,' says Terry. 'There's *no* Santa left standing, so we still don't know which one is real.'

At that moment, I hear the unmistakable sound
of flying cats whooshing through the air, and Jill
zooms down out of the sky in her flying-cat sleigh.

CHAPTER 9

JILL TO THE RESCUE

'Oh my goodness,' says Jill. 'I *love* how you've decorated the tree this year—a twinkling light on every leaf, plastic reindeer hanging from the branches and a huge pile of inflatable Santas! The treehouse looks amazing!'

'Thanks,' I say. 'But they're not decorations—they're *real* reindeer, and *real* Santas!'

'*Real?*' says Jill. 'What do you mean?'

'Well,' I say, 'those reindeer are *actually* Santa's reindeer, and one of the Santas is the *actual* Santa. The others are clones. Santa crashed his sleigh and fell into the cloning machine.'

'And then all the Santas had a big belly bounce-off to see which one of them was the real Santa,' says Terry. 'But they ended up just knocking each other out.'

'But it's Christmas Eve!' says Jill. 'Santa should be out delivering presents.'

'We know,' says Terry.

'The children of the world are going to be so sad if they wake up and find their Christmas stockings empty,' says Jill.

'We know that, too!' I say. 'But what can we do? *We* can't deliver the presents.'

'Why not?' says Jill.

'Because we're not Santa,' I say.

'Where's his sleigh?' says Jill.

'Up there,' says Terry, pointing to where it is teetering dangerously on the edge of the level it crashed on.

lost sausage

'Great!' says Jill. 'And I can see Santa's sack of presents is still in the back. We can deliver them for him.'

'But how will we get all the reindeer out of the tree?' I say. 'Their antlers are all tangled up in the branches.'

'We can grab them with the GRABINATOR,' says Terry. 'It can grab anything from anywhere at any time.'

'But it would have to grab them *very* carefully,' I say, 'and that will take too long.'

'I agree,' says Jill. 'I think we should use my flying cats instead and get the reindeer down later, after we've delivered all the presents.'

'Well, what are we waiting for?' I say. 'Let's go!'

'Hang on a minute,' says Jill. 'We can't deliver presents dressed like this. We need to look more Christmassy.'

'This sounds like a job for the Disguise-o-matic 5000,' I say.

(If you're like most of our readers, you probably know that the Disguise-o-matic 5000 is part of our high-tech detective agency. It has a disguise for every occasion—including a full range of Christmas costumes!)

We climb as fast as we can to the detective agency, go through the extensive security protocols to get in, and head straight to the Disguise-o-matic 5000.

Jill chooses a Santa suit and puts it on. She walks around patting her belly and saying, 'Ho ho ho! Merry Christmas!'

'How come you get to be Santa?' says Terry.

'Well,' says Jill, 'I figure since my cats are pulling the sleigh and I'll be driving, I should be Santa. You two can be my helper elves.'

'I don't want to be a helper elf,' says Terry, who's put on a spiky, armoured suit. 'I'm going to be a helper *orc* instead. RARRRR!'

'There's no such thing as helper orcs!' says Jill. 'Orcs are horrible, not helpful!'

'What about a helper vampire?' says Terry, creeping towards me in a long black cloak.

'I vant to suck your blood!' he says, lunging at my neck with his big fake fangs.

'Quit it!' I say. 'I don't want my blood sucked—and I don't want to be a helper elf any more than you do, but vampires can't deliver presents.'

'Why not?'

'Because it's Christmas, not Halloween!'

'Good point,' says Terry. 'I'll be a helper killer robot instead. KILL! CRUSH! DESTROY!'

'That's even worse, Terry,' says Jill. 'Killing, crushing and destroying isn't going to help us deliver presents—it's just going to make a big mess. Does the Disguise-o-matic 5000 have any helper elf suits?'

stuffing

'Unfortunately, yes,' I say. 'Here they are: one for you, Terry, and one for me.'

We put on our costumes. They are green and red, and the shoes have long curly toes. And, as if that's not bad enough, our hats have ribbons and bells on them.

'We look ridiculous,' I say.

'Look on the bright side,' says Terry. 'At least nobody will see us—they'll all be asleep.'

'Let's hope so,' I say.

'Ho ho ho,' says Jill, practising her Santa laugh again. 'You both look very Christmassy. Come on, let's get going.'

We return to the level where Santa crashed, and pull the sleigh back from the edge.

Terry reaches into the sleigh and pulls out a very long paper scroll. 'Look at this,' he says. 'It's Santa's list.'

cat tail
not lost
sausage

lost
sausage

'That's just what we need,' I say. 'It tells us exactly where to go and who gets which presents.'

'We should get going right away,' says Jill. 'It's almost midnight and we have a lot to do!'

Jill hitches her cats to the sleigh and we all climb in.

'Okay, hold tight, everybody!' says Jill. 'Now, Silky, Scratchy, Scary and Blurry … Tinkerbell, Crashy, Slashy, Trashy and Purry! To the top of the porch … to the top of the wall! Now fly away, fly away, fly away, all! HO HO HO!'

The cats all flap their wings and the sleigh rises
into the air, but then it bumps back down onto
the deck.

BUMP!

'What's the matter?' I say. 'Why aren't we flying?'
   'I think the sleigh is too heavy for my cats,'
says Jill.

'Never fear,' says Terry, pointing. 'Look! Quazjex is here! As well as being a stunt axolotl, he's very strong. He can provide the extra stunt-axolotl sleigh-pulling power we need!'

Hola, Feliz Navidad

Jill attaches Quazjex to the harness alongside Silky and then climbs back into the sleigh.

'Hang on a minute,' I say. 'We can't go yet.
Silky and Quazjex don't have glowing red noses
like Rudolph—we won't be able to see where
we're going!'

'No problem,' says Terry. 'I have an emergency
can of glow-in-the-dark red paint.'

It's not long before Silky and Quazjex's freshly
painted noses are glowing brightly.

'I think we're ready now!' says Jill. 'Now, Silky, Scratchy, Scary and Blurry ... Tinkerbell, Crashy, Slashy, Trashy and Purry—and Quazjex! To the top of the porch ... to the top of the wall! Now fly away, fly away, fly away, all! HO HO HO!'

And up and away we fly into the sky!

CHAPTER 10

AROUND THE WORLD ☆ ✦ ☆

We fly through the air,

Through the dark evening mist,

Delivering presents

To all on the list.

No present too big,

No present too small,

No present too heavy—

We deliver them all.

We put them in pillowslips,

Stockings and sacks.

We arrange them in piles

And towering stacks.

T-shirts and sweaters,

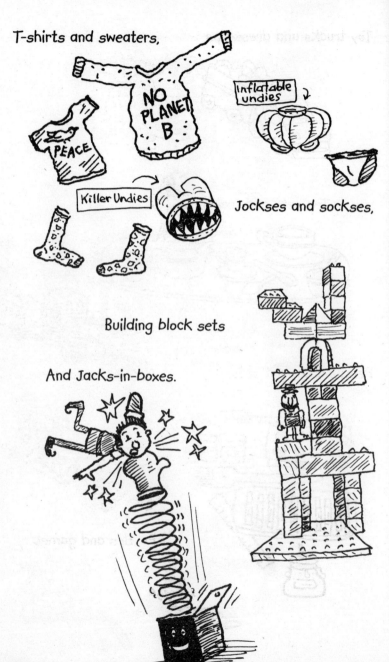

NO PLANET B

PEACE

inflatable undies

Killer Undies

Jockses and sockses,

Building block sets

And Jacks-in-boxes.

Toy trucks and dress-ups,

Tea sets and trains,

Pencils and paint sets,

Puzzles and games.

lost
sausage

We take them to children

In houses and flats,

Houseboats and cottages,

Chalets and shacks.

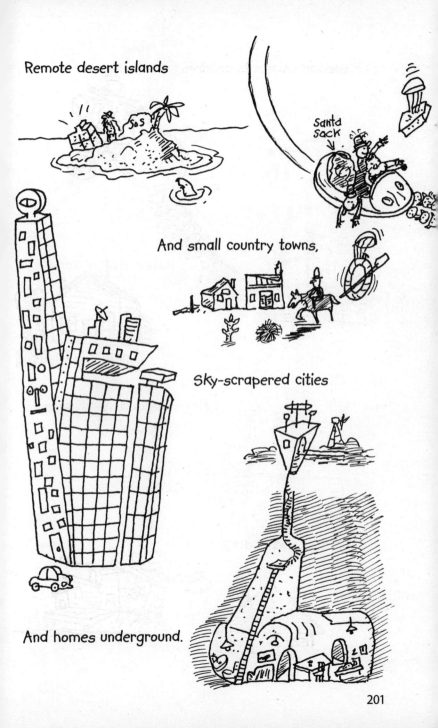

Remote desert islands

And small country towns,

Sky-scrapered cities

And homes underground.

Houses on stilts,

Huts made of bamboo,

Adobes and igloos

Growl!

And treehouses too!

lost sausage

And as we go
We cross off the names:
Georgia and Aysha,
And Henry and James.

HO HO HO

Toby, Sabrina,
Oscar and Pearl,
Jacob and Seo-yun,
Elijah and Earl.

Ivy and Dillon,
Lulu and Mac,
Enya and Evan,
Jasper and Jack.

Casper and Cadence,
Edvard and Lenny,
Jonah and Jules,
Riley and Penny.

Ifemelu and Bjorn,
Astrid and Inger,
Mikael, Anna,
Karl and Kristina.

Lily and Ella,
Eve and Minjun,
Jessica, Daan,
Ji-ho and Ha-joon.

Sem and Milan,
Lotte and Fleur,
Santosh and Sunil,
Billy and Per.

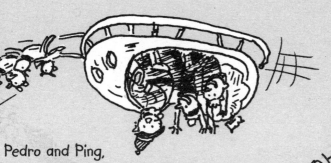

Pedro and Ping,
Olga and Tatyana,
Perry and Ivan,
Derk and Svetlana.

OH OH OHOHOH≡≡≡

Joshua and Samuel,
Giovanni and Mateo,
William and Charlie,
Justine and Theo.

Nahni and Seren,
Otis and Vacha,
Banjo and Dougal,
Kiara and Sasha.

lost sausage

Rafael and Rufus,
Zea and Miuko,
Sylvie and Calilah,
Harun and Haruto.

Ethan and Ian,
Paris and Elle,
Declan, Sofia,
Santiago and Belle.

HO HOHO HO

Finally, we deliver
The very last gift
To the very last child
On Santa's long list—

A shiny new xylophone
For Zoe Zizzerzopolous
(Which, as you can imagine,
Is a great relief for all of us).

And I think to myself,
As daylight draws near,
No wonder Santa does this
Just one time a year!

But, although we're tired,

We are as happy as can be,

For soon it will be Christmas Day

And we'll be back home in our tree.

YAWN!

CHAPTER 11

REINDEER RECOVERY

Jill points the sleigh towards the treehouse. Fortunately, Zoe Zizzerzopolous doesn't live too far from us, so we're home in almost no time.

It's easy to tell our tree apart from all the other trees in the forest. As well as the fact that it has a Christmas light on every leaf, it's the only tree with reindeer in the branches.

Jill lands the sleigh on our observation deck. 'Well, that was fun,' she says. 'Now let's untangle those poor reindeer.'

'I'm on it,' says Terry, jumping into the cockpit of the GRABINATOR. 'I'll set it to super-dainty grabbing so I don't hurt any of them.'

The GRABINATOR daintily grabs Dasher ...

and Dancer and Prancer ...

217

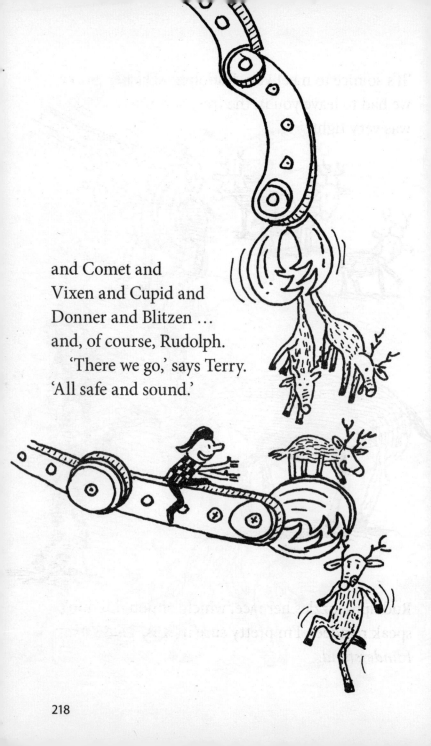

and Comet and
Vixen and Cupid and
Donner and Blitzen …
and, of course, Rudolph.

 'There we go,' says Terry.
'All safe and sound.'

'It's so nice to meet you, Rudolph,' says Jill. 'Sorry we had to leave you in the tree, but time was very tight.'

Rudolph nuzzles her face, which, although I don't speak reindeer, I'm pretty sure means, *That's okay, I understand.*

'Wow,' says Terry. 'That's Rudolph—*Rudolph the Red-nosed Reindeer*!'

'I know,' I say. 'It's so exciting to see such a famous reindeer in the flesh, and look at that nose—it really does glow!'

lost sausage

'It sure does,' says Jill. 'And it's also going to help us identify the real Santa.'

'How?' I say. 'If Quizzy the quizzical quizbot couldn't figure out which one was real, what makes you think a reindeer will be able to do it?'

'Well,' says Jill, 'reindeer have an *excellent* sense of smell. And Rudolph's red nose not only glows, it's also super sensitive. He'll sniff out the true Santa Claus in no time.'

We lead Rudolph to the quiz level, where the
Santas are all still lying in a big pile.

Rudolph walks slowly around the Santas,
sniffing loudly. Finally he stops and nudges one.

The Santa doesn't stir. Rudolph nudges again,
more roughly this time, and licks the Santa's face.

The Santa opens his eyes, blinks, gets to his feet
and gives Rudolph a big hug.

'It's good to see you, Rudolph, you old rascal,'
says Santa. 'Thanks for waking me up. Oh my
goodness, look at the time. We have to get going—
those children need their presents!'

'Relax, Santa,' I say. 'It's all taken care of. Jill, Terry and I delivered the rest of the presents for you.'

'*All* of them?' says Santa.
   'Yes,' says Terry. 'Every last one.'
   'Even Zoe Zizzerzopolous's xylophone?'
   'Of course,' says Jill.

'How can I ever thank you?' says Santa.

'You don't have to thank us at all,' says Terry. 'We had a great time!'

'I'm glad to hear it,' says Santa. 'I'm just sorry I crashed and put you to so much trouble.'

CHOMP!

lost sausage

'The crash wasn't your fault,' I say. 'It was the puddle's.'

'Puddle?' says Jill. 'What puddle?'

'The puddle that used to be the Christmas snowman,' says Terry. 'Andy melted it with a flamethrower.'

'That doesn't sound very Christmassy,' says Santa.

'Well, it wasn't a very Christmassy snowman,' says Terry. 'It threw its head at Andy and then tried to crush us both with its body. You can read all about it in our book.'

'OUR BOOK!' I say. 'We're supposed to deliver it today but we haven't even written it!'

'Why don't we write it now?' says Terry. 'After everything that's happened, we've got a *lot* to write about!'

'You can say that again,' says Jill.

'After everything that's happened, we've got a *lot* to write about!' says Terry.

'We sure have,' I say. 'Let's get started right away.'

CHAPTER 12

HO HO HO!

And so we do.

We write …

and draw …

and draw ...

and write ...

and draw …

and the great Christmas snowball fight begins!

and write …

'How could you possibly have read our books?' I say. 'We only just made you.'

The snowman smiles with its jelly-snake mouth and says, 'My grandmother used to read them to me when I was just a little snowboy.

'That's why I wanted to come here. Your treehouse looked like a lot more fun than standing around freezing my base off in Antarctica.

'So I packed myself in a box and mailed myself here. I knew you two chuckleheads wouldn't be able to resist making a snowman out of a box of snow. And so, here I am!

'Don't forget to shut the door on your way out,' he says. 'Actually, on second thoughts, leave it open. It's quite warm in here. I think it's all those Christmas lights you've hung everywhere. Where's the off switch?'

Says Andy smiling. said Andy, with his hair on fire.

and write …

Rudolph the red-nose eleph ant.

and draw …

and write …

'Quit it!' I say. 'I don't want my blood sucked—and I don't want to be a helper elf any more than you do, but vampires can't deliver presents.'

'Why not?'

'Because it's Christmas, not Halloween!'

'Good point,' says Terry. 'I'll be a helper killer robot instead. KILL! CRUSH! DESTROY!'

KILL! CRUSH! DESTROY!

184

'That's even worse, Terry,' says Jill. 'Killing, crushing and destroying isn't going to help us deliver presents—it's just going to make a big mess. Does the Disguise-o-matic 5000 have any helper elf suits?'

stuffing

'Unfortunately, yes,' I say. 'Here they are: one for you, Terry, and one for me.'

185

and write …

Finally, we deliver
The very last gift
To the very last child
On Santa's long list—

ZOE

A shiny new xylophone
For Zoe Zizzerzopolous
(Which, as you can imagine,
Is a great relief for all of us).

And I think to myself,
As daylight draws near,
No wonder Santa does this
Just one time a year!

lost sausage

210

211

and draw …

and draw …

and write and write until it's all finished.

YET ANOTHER END

The book ↓

What a lovely picture.

the characters

We're all looking at the book!

'I'm glad that's done,' says Terry. 'Now all we have
to do is get it to Mr Big Nose.'

'I can drop it off on my way back to the North
Pole,' says Santa. 'It can be his Christmas present.'

'Thanks, Santa!' I say. 'But Mr Big Nose doesn't
believe in Christmas.'

'Oh, we'll see about that,' says Santa, smiling.

Santa hitches his reindeer to the sleigh and climbs in. 'Merry Christmas!' he booms as he whooshes off. We all wave goodbye.

We use the telescope on our observation deck to follow Santa's flight to Big Nose Books.

HO HO HO

HO HO HO

HO

SM A
NOS
BOO

We see Santa land on the roof of Big Nose Books and squeeze himself—and our manuscript—down the chimney. (Fortunately, our telescope has a long-range microphone as well so we can listen in.)

'Ho ho ho!' says Santa as he climbs out of the fireplace. 'Merry Christmas, Mr Big Nose!'

'Who the dickens are you?' splutters Mr Big Nose. 'And what do you mean by bursting into my office like this and covering everything in a cloud of soot?'

'I'm Santa Claus,' says Santa. 'And I've brought you a present.'

'A present?' says Mr Big Nose. 'I haven't got time for presents—I'm a busy man!'

lost sausage

'But it's Christmas Day.'

'I don't care what day it is,' says Mr Big Nose. 'I'm busy! And I'm *definitely* too busy for presents.'

'I don't think you're too busy for *this* one,' says
Santa. 'It's from Andy and Terry.'

'Well, why didn't you say so?' says Mr Big Nose,
snatching it off Santa. 'It's *exactly* what I wanted—
but how did you know that?'

'Oh, I know a lot about presents!' says Santa.

'What did you say your name was again?'
says Mr Big Nose.

'Santa,' says Santa. 'Santa Claus.'

'*The* Santa Claus?' says Mr Big Nose.

'The one and only!' says Santa.

'I thought you were just a made-up storybook
character.'

'Oh, I hope not,' says Santa, chuckling and
patting his big round belly.

'Is it true that you fly around and deliver presents to children all over the world in a single night?' says Mr Big Nose.

'Yes,' says Santa. 'Every Christmas Eve. I spend the rest of the year in my North Pole workshop making toys with the elves.'

'My goodness,' says Mr Big Nose. 'And I thought *I* was busy! I think we have a lot in common, you and me. Would you like a drink?'

'Milk, please,' says Santa.

'With ice?' says Mr Big Nose.

'No thanks, there's more than enough ice where I'm going—ho ho ho!'

'Have you ever considered writing a book about your life?' says Mr Big Nose.

'Funny you should ask,' says Santa. 'I've just finished doing exactly that. It's called *The Story of the Autobiography of My Life by Me, Santa, and the True Meaning of Christmas.*'

'Great title!' says Mr Big Nose. 'I'd love to read it.'

'As a matter of fact, I have a copy right here,' says
Santa. He pulls it out from inside his jacket and
hands it to Mr Big Nose. 'I was about to start
looking for a publisher.'

The Story of the Autobiography of My Life by Me, Santa, and the True Meaning of Christmas

lost sausage

'Well, you've just found one,' says Mr Big Nose.
'*Two* books in one day … it's beginning to feel a lot
like Christmas here at Big Nose Books!'

'That's because it *is* Christmas,' says Santa.

'Would you like another glass of milk?' says
Mr Big Nose.

'No, I have to be getting back to the North Pole,'
says Santa, heading for the chimney. 'Mrs Claus
and the elves are expecting me for Christmas lunch.'

'Then I wish you a very Merry Christmas,' says
Mr Big Nose. 'And thanks for the book—I mean,
books!'

'Merry Christmas to you, too!' calls Santa,
as he disappears up the chimney.

'I'm glad that all worked out so well,' says Terry.
'But after a night of delivering presents, I'm
really hungry.'

'Me too,' says Jill. 'Let's get ready for lunch.
Everyone will be here soon.'

'Not so fast,' says a voice. 'We have unfinished business.'

CHAPTER 13

THE LAST CHAPTER

We look down. Yep, you guessed it. It's the puddle.

'How interesting!' says Jill, crouching down to study it more closely. 'A talking puddle!'

'That's the one we were telling you about,' says
Terry. 'The not-very-Christmassy snowman puddle.
I wouldn't get too close if I were you. It's not very
nice *and* it's vowed never-ending revenge on us.'

But before Jill can move away, the puddle rises up,
grabs her around the waist and drags her in.

'Let me go!' yells Jill.

'Not until Andy and Terry agree to get out of
my treehouse!' it yells back.

'*That's* not going to happen,' I say. 'Let her go, or we'll stomp you so hard you'll be nothing but water vapour!'

'Stomp me and you'll stomp Jill!' says the puddle. 'And you don't want that, do you?'

'No, I don't,' I say. 'That does it. Now you've gone too far.'

'Not as far as you're going,' replies the puddle. 'Now hurry up and leave, or I'll drown your little animal-loving pal here!'

'You won't be drowning anybody and we're not going anywhere,' says Terry. 'In fact, it's *you* who's leaving—and very soon, too.'

Terry grabs our endlessly expandable Christmas stockings from the fireplace and throws one to me.

lost sausage

'Ooh, I'm so *scared* of your stockings,' says the puddle sarcastically.

'You should be!' says Terry. 'These endlessly expandable Christmas stockings are also *endlessly super absorbent*! Goodbye—or should I say, Good*DRY*—forever!'

Terry throws his stocking onto the puddle and I do the same.

The stockings immediately begin to soak up the puddle. It gets smaller …

carrot.

and smaller …

and smaller …

'You'll pay for this, you stinking, puddle-shrinking fiends!' says the now-tiny puddle. 'You haven't heard the last of me!'

'Actually, I think we have,' I say as the last drop is absorbed and Jill is left lying safe and sound on the now perfectly dry carpet.

'Yay!' says Jill, jumping to her feet. 'I'm not only free but I'm completely dry as well—those stockings really work! Thank you!'

'Don't mention it,' says Terry. 'That's what friends—and endlessly expandable super-absorbent Christmas stockings—are for!'

'I'm glad the stockings were useful for getting rid of that horrible snowman's puddle,' says Terry. 'But I'm a bit sad that they weren't filled with presents, like we'd hoped.'

'Yeah,' I say. 'We didn't get *any presents at all*. Santa forgot about us!'

'I don't think that's true,' says Jill. 'Look over there, beside the fireplace!'

We look.

Jill's right.

There are three large presents! One for Terry, one for Jill and one for me.

'Santa didn't forget after all!' says Terry.

'Let's open them' I say.

'I can't wait to see what we got.'

'Wow!' says Terry. 'I got an electric pony!'

'Me too!' I say.

Pat!
Pat!

'So did I!' says Jill.

'I'm going to call mine *Lightning*,' says Terry.

'I'm going to call mine *Flashdrive*,' I say.

'I'm going to call mine *Apple Dumpling*,' says Jill.

'*Apple Dumpling*?' I say. 'What sort of name is that for an electric pony?'

'It's a really *good* name,' says Jill. 'I got it out of this book: *Really Good Names for Electric Ponies*.'

'Let's take them for a ride!' I say.

I jump on *Flashdrive* and flick the starter switch. He roars into life.

'WAIT!' says Jill. 'What about lunch? All my animals have been *so* looking forward to it. In fact, they'll be arriving any minute now.'

'Of course,' I say. 'You're absolutely right. Christmas lunch first, electric-pony flying second. Terry, can you set the table for an extra three electric ponies and all the Santa clones, and let Edward Scooperhands know that we're going to need at least 50 times more ice-cream?'

'Sure thing, Andy,' says Terry. 'This is going to be the best Christmas ever!'

'*Going* to be?' I say. 'It already is!'

'Oh no,' I say. 'It's Mr Big Nose—what could he possibly want? He's already got our book!'

'Yeah, leave us alone, you big old poopy head!' says Terry.

'Shush!' I whisper to Terry. 'He might hear you!'
   But it's too late.

↰ Hawaiian shirt

'I beg your pardon, Terry?!' says Mr Big Nose. 'Did
you just call me a *big old poopy head*?'

'Yes,' says Terry quickly. 'But only because Andy *told* me to say it.'

'No I didn't!' I say.

'Did!' says Terry.

'Didn't!' I say.

'It's okay,' says Mr Big Nose. 'It doesn't matter who said it. I'm afraid I have been a bit of a big old poopy head and I'm calling to apologise … and to wish you all a very Merry Christmas!'

'But I thought you didn't believe in Christmas,' I say.

'I didn't,' he says. 'Not until I met Santa and read his book. I now see I was wrong. There's a time for work and a time for play and *definitely* a time for Christmas, which is why I have all of my family here at Big Nose Books for the first annual Big Nose Books Christmas party!'

QUACK!

The filing monster taps Mr Big Nose on the shoulder. 'Excuse me, Mr Big Nose,' he says. 'I'm going to need a bigger P-drawer ... for all these presents!'

'I have to go,' says Mr Big Nose. 'I've got a P-drawer emergency on my hands! Have a very busy—I mean, have a very *Merry* Christmas ... OR ELSE!'

'Merry Christmas to you, too, Mr Poopy—oops—
I mean Mr *Big Nose*!' says Terry.

    'Don't worry about it,' I say. 'He's already gone,
but everybody else is here. Let's turn on the
sandwich machine and get this party started!'

'This is so much fun!' says Terry. 'I wish it could be Christmas every day.'

'Me too,' I say. 'Hey, I know—let's build a Santa Land level for all the Santa clones to live in. Then we can have Christmas whenever we feel like it.'

'If you're adding more levels,' says Jill, 'can one be a stable with fast-charging stations and automatic hoof polishers for our electric ponies?'

'Of course,' I say. 'And speaking of electric ponies, let's take them for a spin before they eat too many Christmas sandwiches and get too full to fly.'

lost sausage

'Yay!' says Terry. 'Up, up and away!'

Lots of laughs

at every level!

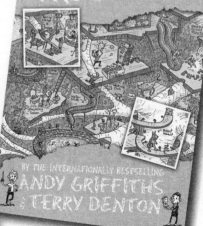

Lots of laughs

at every level!

Lots of laughs

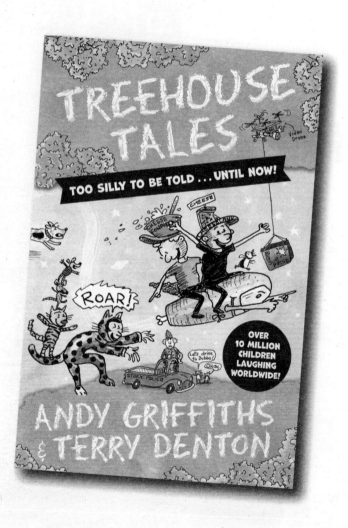

at every level!

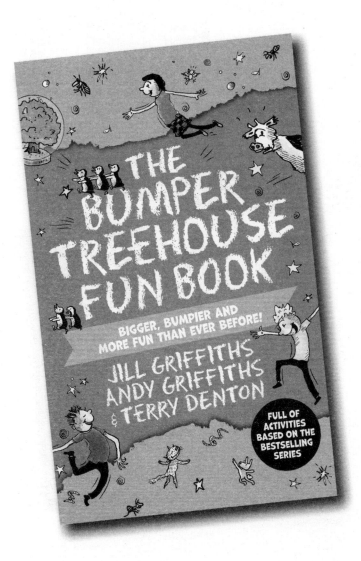

Lots of laughs

FULL OF ACTIVITIES BASED ON THE BESTSELLING SERIES

at every level!

lost
sausage